THE VERY IMPATIENT CATERPILLAR

Ross Burach

Scholastic Press   New York

WAIT?!
You're telling me I can become a BUTTERFLY?
Yes.
With wings?
Yes.
For REAL?
Yes.
Wait for ME!!

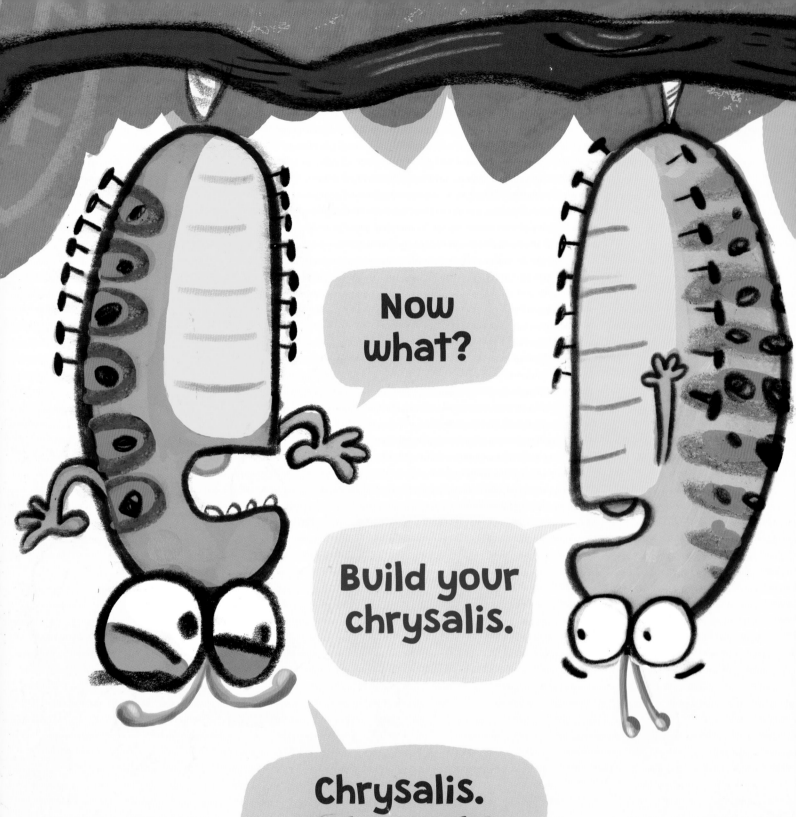

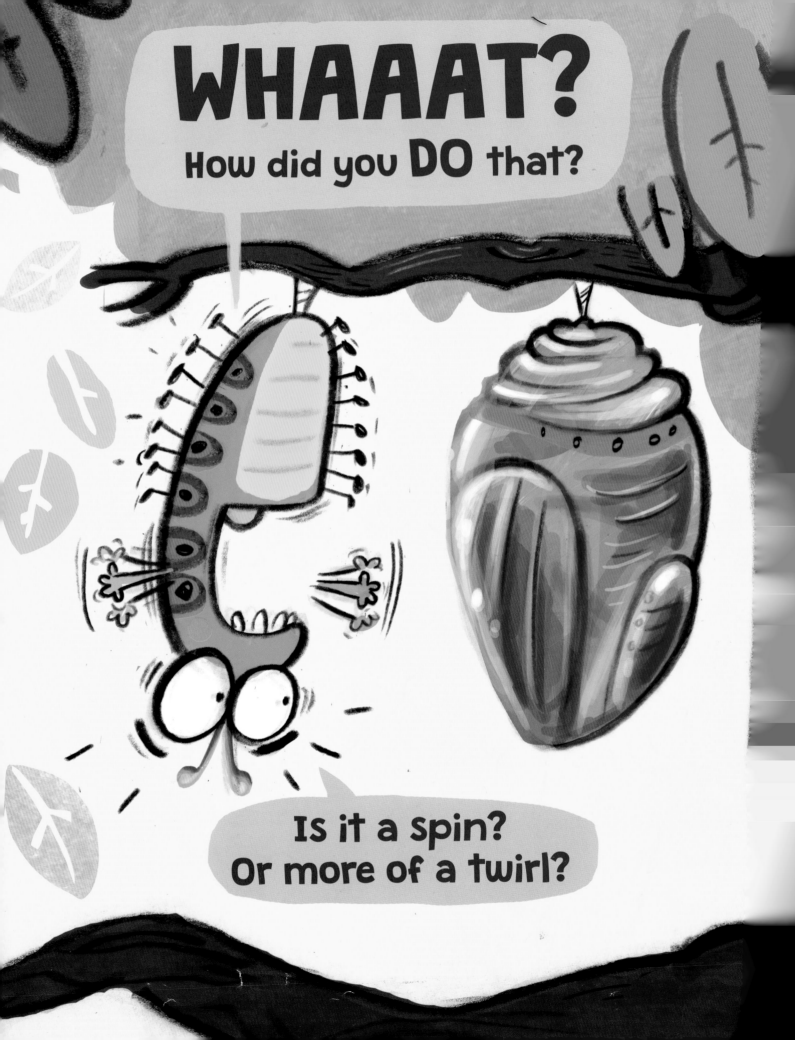

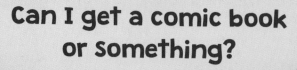

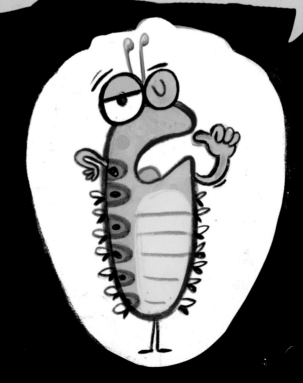

WAIT!!!

Where are my wings?

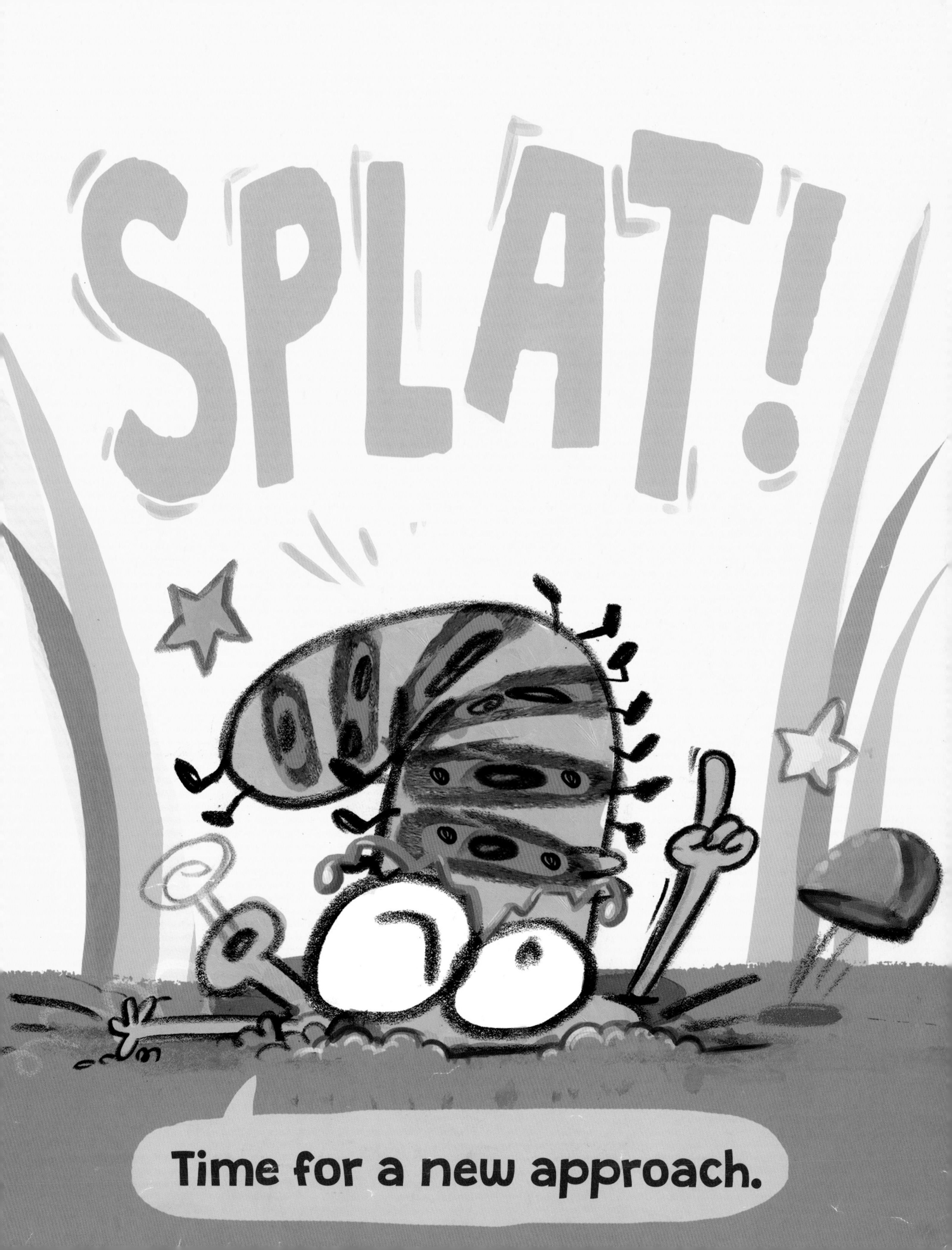
SPLAT!
Time for a new approach.

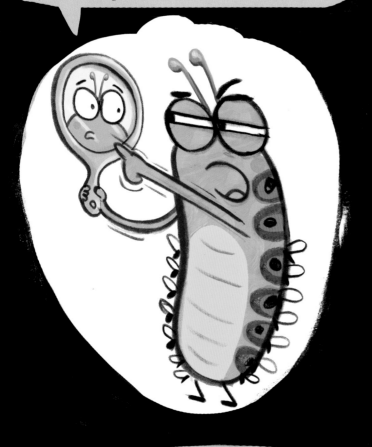

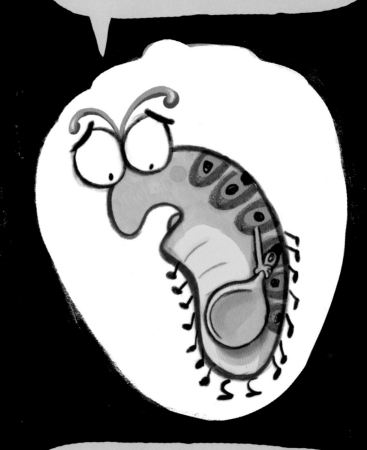

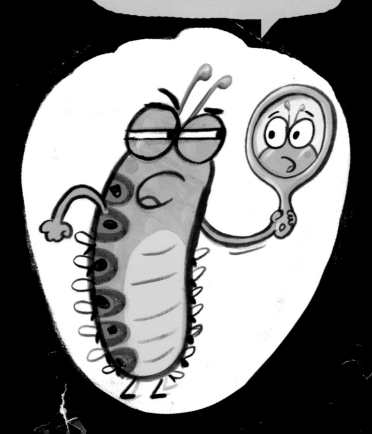

Day 1

Day 2

Day 3

Day 7

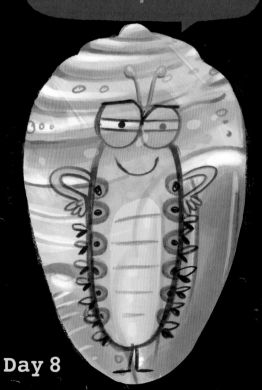

Day 8

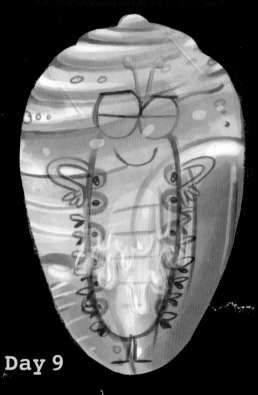

Day 9

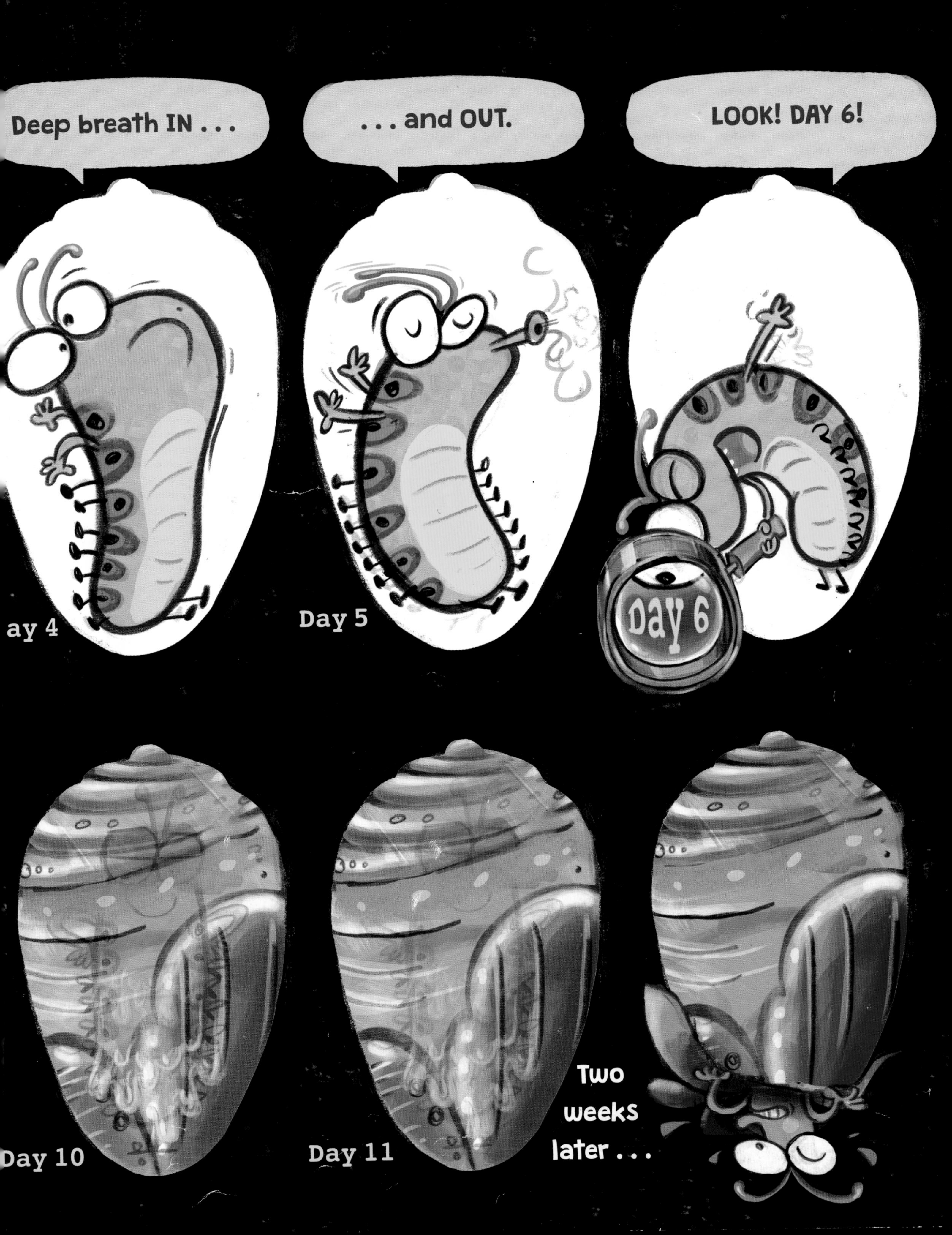
Deep breath IN . . .
. . . and OUT.
LOOK! DAY 6!
ay 4
Day 5
DAY 6
Day 10
Day 11
Two weeks later . . .

I did it! I'm a

BUTTERFLY!

For Mom, thank you
for always being so patient.